The Grandpa Book

TODD PARR

Megan Tingley Books
LITTLE, BROWN AND COMPANY
New York ⋅ Boston

ALSO BY TODD PARR:

The Grandma Book

The Daddy Book

The Mommy Book

The Family Book

It's Okay to Be Different

The Peace Book

The Feel Good Book

Reading Makes You Feel Good

Underwear Do's and Don'ts

Otto Goes to Bed

Otto Goes to the Beach

Otto Goes to Camp

Otto Has a Birthday Party

Otto Goes to School

A complete list of all Todd's titles and
more information can be found at www.toddparr.com

Little, Brown and Company

Time Warner Book Group
1271 Avenue of the Americas, New York, NY 10020
Visit our Web site at www.lb-kids.com

First Edition: April 2006

Library of Congress Cataloging-in-Publication Data

Parr, Todd.
   The grandpa book / by Todd Parr. — 1st ed.
      p. cm.
   "Megan Tingley Books"
   Summary: Presents the different ways grandfathers show their
grandchildren love, from putting extra marshmallows in hot chocolate
to sending cards and telling stories.
   ISBN 0-316-05801-7
   [1. Grandfathers—Fiction. 2. Grandparent and child—Fiction.] I. Title.
PZ7.P2447Gra 2006
[E]—dc22   2004027847

10 9 8 7 6 5 4 3 2 1

TWP

Printed in Singapore

This book is dedicated to my Grandpa Parr, who wasn't around long enough. Thanks for helping me draw.

And to my Grandpa Logan, who taught me how to fish and plant a garden. Thanks for forgiving me for all those soda cans I used to stuff under the cushion of your favorite chair.

 Love,
Todd

Some grandpas collect a lot of different things

Some grandpas have a lot of pictures of you

Some grandpas put extra money in your piggy bank

Some grandpas put extra marshmallows in your hot chocolate

All grandpas like to

tell you stories

Some grandpas talk really loudly

Some grandpas send you cards

Some grandpas can wiggle their ears

Some grandpas let you
try on their glasses

make you laugh

Some grandpas take you to school

Some grandpas take you to the park.

Some grandpas live with a grandma

Some grandpas live with their friends

Some grandpas like to walk

Some grandpas like to drive

All grandpas like to

hold and hug you

Grandpas are very special. They make you laugh and teach you new things. Be sure to tell them how much you love them.

♡ Love, Todd